The Legend of Toe Jam Joe

Scott James Peterson

The Legend of
Toe Jam Joe

Scott James Peterson

This book is dedicated to Jaimie, Spencer, Brennan, Claudia, Mum & Dad, and the rest of my family for their unwavering support. Also, to Kerrie who has been waiting so patiently over the past year for Toe Jam Joe to come to life.

I love you all and Thank you.

In Loving Memory of:

"Auntie" Paula Paul
January 25th, 1943 – February 28th, 2017

The Toe Jam Joe Concept, Story, Characters, and Song were created by me, but would not have been possible with out my daughter's curiousity.

ISBN-13: 978-0692083475 (Peterson Productions)

© 2014, 2018 Copyright   Scott James Peterson
All Rights reservered. Unlawful duplication without permission is a violation of applicable laws.

All images were painted in watercolour and edited with Photoshop.
Fonts: Adler Regular, 69 Regular AR DECODE Regular, Courier New Regular,
Black Chancery Regular, and Tabatha Normal.

www.scottjamespeterson.com

Download and listen to "The Legend of Toe Jam Joe" song available now online.
Visit www.scottjamespeterson.com for more details on where to find it.

Toe Jam Joe likes to roam around,

through the farms and fields,
and the towns that surround.

He likes the squish of the jelly
up under his feet.

He likes to yip
and yollar,

hoot and hollar.

You can hear him singing
for a mile and a quarter.

Singing about his jelly
that is ever so sweet.

Now, no one knows when he first came around...

some say he came
from a mushroom,

he came from
the ground.

And all the kids believe he
was born from unicorn pooh.

Now, all the kids love to follow him around, when Old Jelly Joe comes to town...

They all want a taste of his
jelly that is so yummy to eat.

Toe Jam Joe... Toe Jam Joe

The funny old man with jelly between his toes.

Toe Jam Joe... Toe Jam Joe

The funny old man with the rainbows between his toes.

He carries a loaf of bread in his sack, with peanut butter,

he will make you a nice snack.

Spreading that jelly oozing from out of his feet.

Between the first few toes
you'll find RED and GREEN,
from the strawberry fields
and the spearmint leaves

And the ORANGE marmalade,
well,.. no one knows
why it glows.

The **BLUE** is from blueberries, and the **PURPLE** one is from grape jelly,

And the PINK raspberry is more tart than it is sweet.

Now the strangest flavor
is the YELLOW one,
made from dandilions,
made with the sun

And the apple is such a GOLDEN delicious treat.

Toe Jam Joe... Toe Jam Joe

The funny old man with
jelly between his toes.

Toe Jam Joe... Toe Jam Joe

The funny old man with the rainbow between his toes.

to share his jelly with everyone that he greets.

Well, the folks whispers,
they got louder.

They started to snit.

They started to hollar.

Yelling at Joe to drive him
from out of their streets.

Disturbed by the ruckus the Mayor ran out,

but wound up with a toe full in his mouth.

He then proclaimed that he had never tasted anything so sweet.

He praised Joe with
the key to the town,

the kids all sang and
danced around

Singing about his jelly
and his magical feet.

Toe Jam Joe...

Toe Jam Joe

The funny old man with jelly between his toes.

Toe Jam Joe... Toe Jam Joe

The funny old man with the rainbows between his toes.

Toe Jam Joe...

Toe Jam Joe

The funny old man
with rainbows between his toes.

The funny old man with
jelly between his toes.

The funny old man with jelly between his toes.

The Legend of
Toe Jam Joe

Inspired by Ron Peterson Jr, my beautiful daughter Claudia, and fruit flavored candies.

Yummy.

February 22, 1965- July 15, 2001

THE LEGEND OF TOE JAM JOE first came to life one night back in 2014 when my daughter, who was 5 years old at the time, had just finished her nightly bath. While drying her feet she began playing with her toes and she asked me, "Daddy, where does toe jam come from?" While holding back my giggles at her extreme cuteness, I decided to have a little fun with her. Playing off of a name that my late brother Ronnie used to call *Mike and Ike* candies; Toe Jam Jelly Joe's, I proceeded to make up a story about a funny old man named Toe Jam Joe,and his magical feet filled with jelly. The story quickly turned into a silly little song and we started dancing and stomping around her room singing *"Toe Jam Joe... Toe Jam Joe. The funny old man with jelly between his toes"*. The song was so catchy, it was stuck in my head for days. A few years later I decided to record the song and turn Toe Jam Joe into a picture book to share with the rest of the world. Why is Joe designed after a Mountain Man? Well, My brother and I would frequently attend Mountain Man Rendezvous, so I wanted to pay homage to him for inspiring the name of this book. I decided to use Ronnie's Mountain Man outfit for the premise of Joes look.

Even though your gone Ronnie, you still inspire and make us laugh.

We miss you.

www.scottjamespeterson.com

Made in the USA
Middletown, DE
13 April 2022

63827212R00024